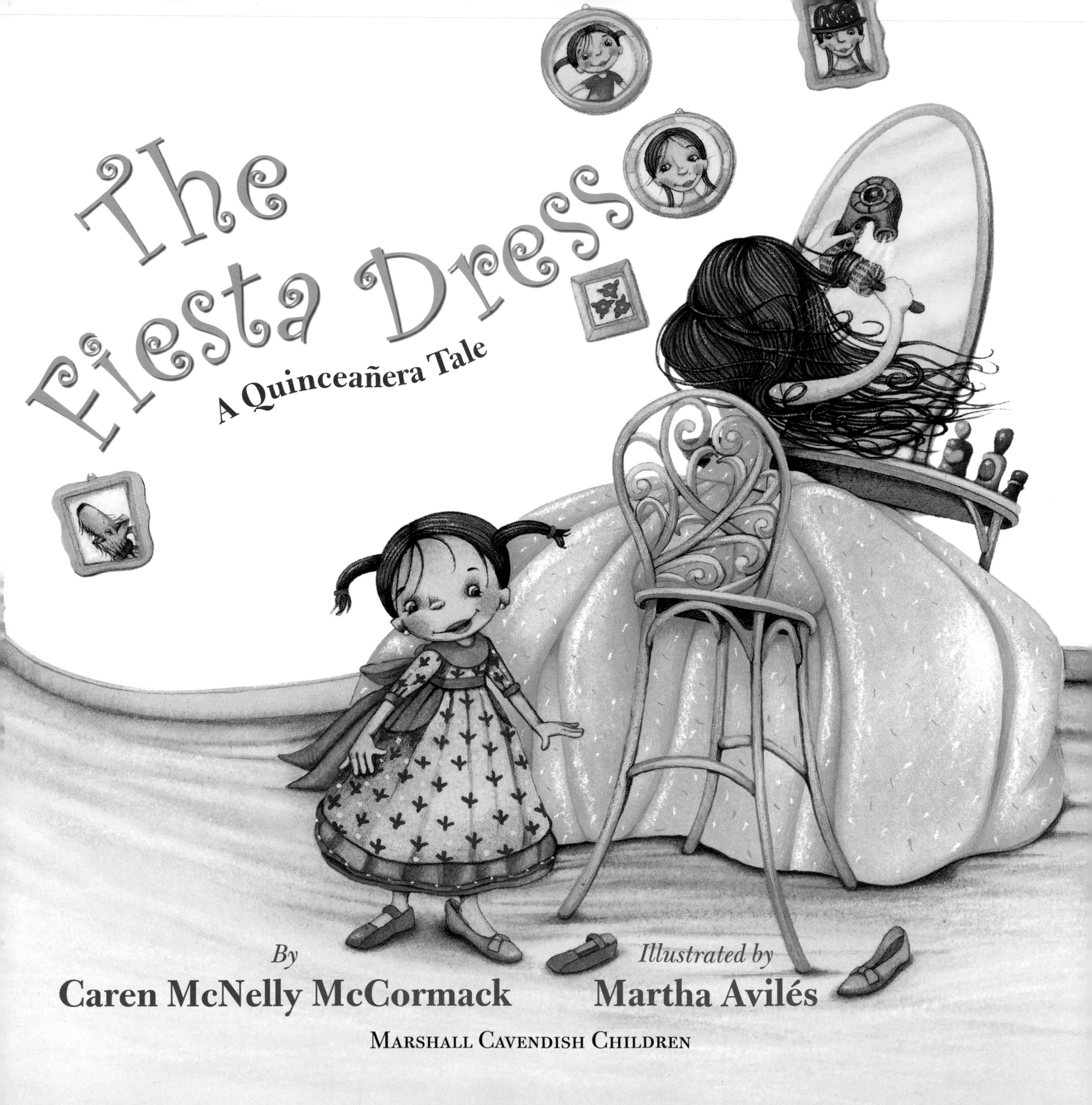
The Fiesta Dress
A Quinceañera Tale
By
Caren McNelly McCormack
Illustrated by
Martha Avilés
Marshall Cavendish Children

Marshall Cavendish Corporation
99 White Plains Road, Tarrytown, NY 10591
www.marshallcavendish.us/kids

Library of Congress Cataloging-in-Publication Data
McNelly McCormack, Caren.
The fiesta dress : a quinceañera tale / by Caren McNelly McCormack; illustrated by Martha Aviles. — 1st ed.
p. cm.
Summary: While Eva and her family prepare for her quinceañera, no one is paying attention to her younger sister, but when the dog gets out of the laundry room and steals Eva's sash, her little sister comes to the rescue.
ISBN 978-0-7614-5467-0
[1. Quinceañera (Social custom)—Fiction. 2. Sisters—Fiction. 3. Family life—Southwest, New—Fiction. 4. Hispanic Americans—Fiction. 5. Southwest, New—Fiction.] I. Avilés Junco, Martha, ill. II. Title.
PZ7.M2355Fi 2009
[E]—dc22
2008010781

The illustrations were rendered in acrylics and
liquid watercolor on Arches paper.
Book design by Vera Soki
Editor: Marilyn Mark

Printed in China
First edition
1 3 5 6 4 2
mc Marshall Cavendish Children

For Jon and J.C., both givers of good gifts

—C.M.M.

For Renata and Miranda

—M.A.

When you are the baby of the family everyone notices you.

THE NEWS
THE NEWS
THE NEWS

Mamá and Papá clap when I pirouette my best ballerina twirls.

My big sister Eva cheers
when I race to the end of the block.

The neighbors gasp when I climb to the top of the pecan tree before anyone can stop me.

"Lolo," Papá says, "you're always on the move."

"With fast feet like yours," Mamá says, "it's hard to keep up."

But while everyone prepared for Eva's *quinceañera*, no one noticed me.

The *damas* didn't as they swished and swirled in their bright dresses. They whirred, curled, brushed, and combed as they dressed for the *fiesta*. They never saw me patting clouds of powder on my face.

In the kitchen, no one noticed me. The *tías* didn't as they scooped, patted, wrapped, and tied, making the biggest batch of tamales ever. They never saw me slipping one into my pocket.

In the backyard, no one noticed me. The *tíos* didn't as they unraveled, tossed, tugged, and twisted strands of lights over the patio and through the trees. They never saw me swinging from the pecan tree.

In the den, the *primos* didn't notice me. They huffed, puffed, whistled, and cheered at the video game. They never saw me practicing handstands against the wall.

Even Gobi, the *perro*, didn't notice me. He sighed, snuffled, scratched, and shook when I let him out of the laundry room. He flew past me and bounded upstairs before I could throw him his favorite squeaky toy.

But everyone noticed when—"AHHHH!"—Eva shrieked from the bedroom. The blow-dryers hushed. The pots piped down. The backyard lights fizzled. Even the video game clicked off.

"Gobi took my sash!" Eva screamed. "That drooling dog took my perfect white sash. My *quinceañera* dress is ruined!"

C-H

Mamá and Papá bolted to the laundry room.

"Where is that dog?" Papá moaned.

"How did Gobi get out?" Mamá wailed.

I gulped. I didn't want them to notice me now. I slipped out the door to look for Gobi.

I found Gobi at the corner with the sash in his clenched teeth.
"It looks like we're both in the doghouse," I said to him. "Give me the sash."
Gobi flicked his ears and clamped his teeth tighter.

“Come on.” I popped my hands on my hips. I felt a lump in my pocket. Aha! I knew just how to save Eva’s sash.

"Who makes the best tamales on the planet?" I asked Gobi. I slid off the corn husk wrapper and dangled the tamale above him.

Gobi cocked his head.

"My *tías*!" I said and flipped the tamale into the air.

Gobi dropped the sash and leaped up for a bite.

Before his teeth closed on the tamale, I snatched the sash and dashed for home.

Mamá, Papá, and Eva met me at the door.

"I'm sorry I let out Gobi," I said. "I just wanted someone to play with me."

"You weren't using your head when you opened the laundry room door," Papá said.

"But at least you used your head and your feet to set the problem straight," Mamá said.

“I’m glad to have my sash back,” Eva said as she brushed some dirt from my cheek. “But I’m even happier to have my special sister with me on my big day.”

Eva pecked each of my cheeks. “*Besitos, besitos*,” she said.

I beamed and spread my arms in a deep ballet bow.

Then everyone noticed me.

The *damas* did. They swept me into Eva's room and twined my hair with ribbons. They straightened my dress and swabbed my shoes.

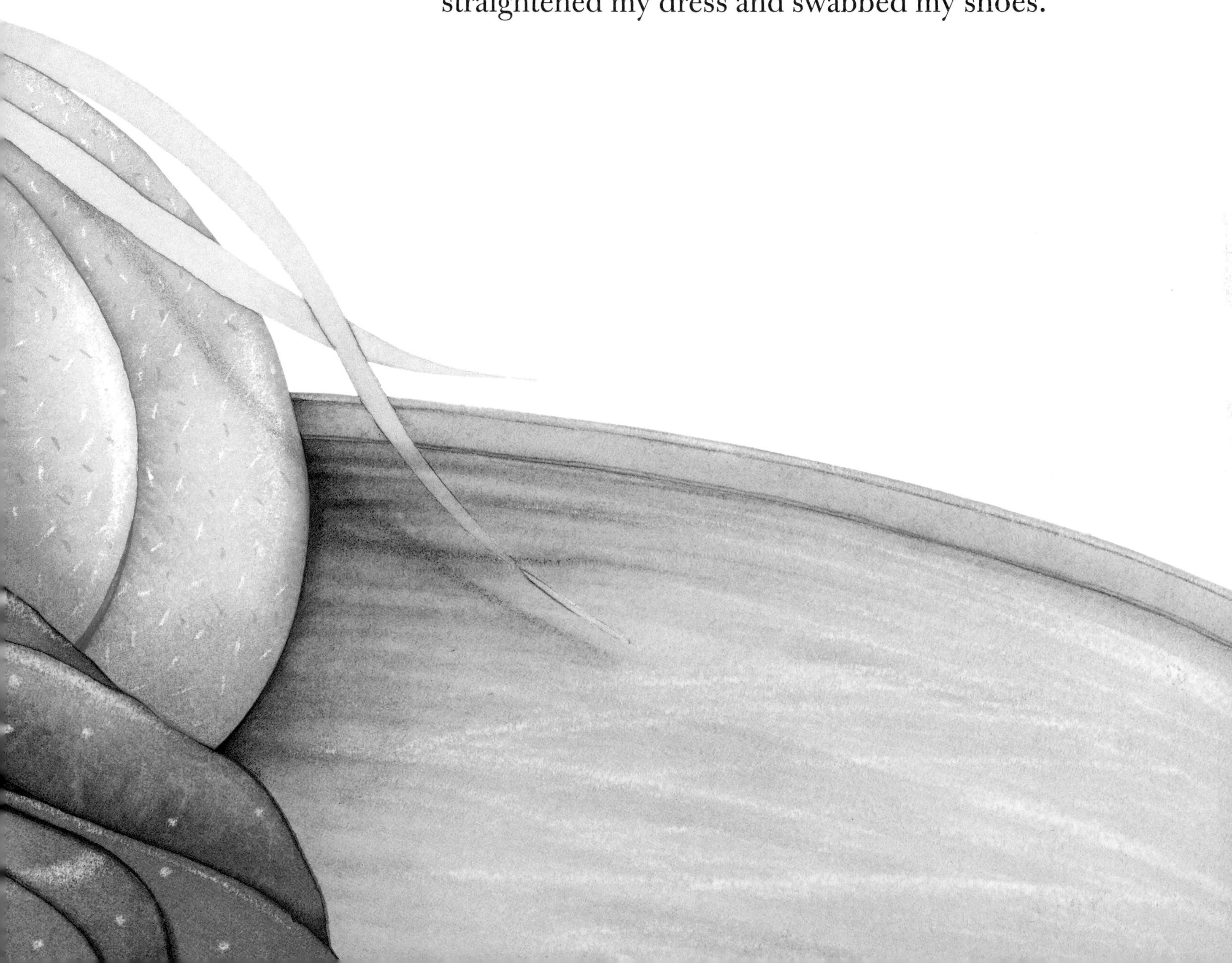

The *tías* noticed me. They hustled me into the kitchen and handed me the fattest tamale on a plate. They squeezed and kissed me while I ate by the stove.

The *tíos* noticed me, too. They whisked me to the backyard and spun me in a *baile* under the twinkling lights.

They lifted me so I could swing from a high tree branch.

Even the *primos* clicked off the game in the den. They showered me with high fives and peppered me with questions.

And for the rest of the day, while everyone celebrated Eva's big *fiesta*,

Gobi and I whirled, munched, jumped, skipped, hummed, giggled, hollered, and grinned.

Glossary

Baile—Dance. *Quinceañera* parties often include special dances performed by the *quinceañera* girl and her attendants. After the choreographed dancing, the dance floor opens to all the guests.

Besitos—Kisses or, literally, little kisses

Damas—The *quinceañera* girl's female attendants, similar to bridesmaids. The *damas* are typically sisters, cousins, or friends. In a traditional *quinceañera*, fourteen *damas*, fourteen *chambelanes*, or male attendants, and a man of honor accompany the girl.

Fiesta—Party

Perro—Dog

Primos—Cousins

Quinceañera—Refers to both the girl and the event of the traditional celebration of a girl's 15th birthday held in many Latin countries and by Latinos in the United States. It marks a girl's change to womanhood. The *quinceañera* event has two parts: a Mass honoring the girl's commitment to the Church and a large party for friends and family. The party usually includes music and food and is held in a home or rented space. The *quinceañera* girl wears a full, formal dress, similar to a wedding gown, and her attendants wear colored formal gowns that complement the color of her dress.

Tías—Aunts

Tíos—Uncles